LOBO
AND THE
RABBIT STEW
El lobo y el caldo de conejo

Written by/Escrito por **Marcia Schwartz**
Illustrated by/Ilustrado por **D. B. Campbell**

For Lucy, my granddaughter and *compañera* in "spinning" stories. — MS
For my kids, Thomas and Kate. — BC

Text ©2010 by Marcia Schwartz
Illustration ©2010 by D. B. Campbell
Translation ©2010 Raven Tree Press

Schwartz, Marcia.

Lobo and the rabbit stew / written by Marcia Schwartz; illustrated by D. B. Campbell; translated by Cambridge BrickHouse = El lobo y el caldo de conejo / escrito por Marcia Schwartz; ilustrado por D. B. Campbell; traducción al español de Cambridge BrickHouse —1 ed. —McHenry, IL : Raven Tree Press, 2010.

p. ; cm.

SUMMARY: Lobo the wolf attempts to outwit Bunny to put him in a stew, but Bunny outsmarts the wolf. A retelling of The Three Little Pigs.

Bilingual Edition
ISBN 978-1-936299-00-3 hardcover
ISBN 978-1-936299-01-0 paperback

English-only Edition
ISBN 978-1-936299-002-7 hardcover

Audience: pre-K to 3rd grade
Title available in English-only or bilingual English-Spanish editions

1. Fairy Tales & Folklore / Adaptations —Juvenile fiction. 2. Animals / Wolves & Coyotes—Juvenile fiction. 3. Bilingual books—English and Spanish. 4. [Spanish language materials-books.] I. Illust. Campbell, Brent. II. Title. III. Title: El lobo y el caldo de conejo

LCCN: 2010922814

Printed in Taiwan
10 9 8 7 6 5 4 3 2 1
First Edition

Free activities for this book are available at www.raventreepress.com

Raven Tree Press
A Division of Delta Systems Co., Inc.
www.raventreepress.com

As the moon rose over the canyon,
el señor Lobo crawled from his cave.

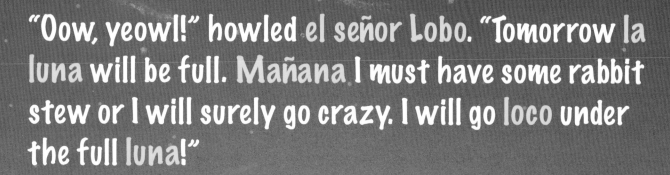

"Oow, yeowl!" howled el señor Lobo. "Tomorrow la luna will be full. Mañana I must have some rabbit stew or I will surely go crazy. I will go loco under the full luna!"

Lobo's howling echoed through the canyon. Little Conejito Bunny hid under a blanket in the burrow. "Do you hear that howling?" asked Mama. "El lobo needs a tender young bunny for his conejo stew. You must stay here in la madriguera until the full moon passes." Conejito nodded and hid under his manta once more.

"Mañana I must go down into the valley to help your grandmother pick lettuce," said Mama.

"While I am helping your abuela, you must not go out of the burrow or let anyone in. Do you understand?" "¿Comprendes?" she asked again. "Sí," whispered Conejito. "Yes, I understand," he said.

Early in the morning, Mama Rabbit
hopped off to Abuela's burrow.

Conejito was busy having fun. Before long, he heard a knock on the door. He remembered what Mama had said. He did not go to la puerta.

"Hello, my little friend," said the wolf. "Hola, mi pequeño amigo," he repeated. "I know you are in there, so let me in," cooed el señor Lobo.

"Go away! ¡Vete!" shouted Conejito. "Mama is coming back soon and she will make a fur coat out of you!"

"Ah, don't be afraid of me, Bebé. I just want to give you a treat. It is so delicious! ¡Muy delicioso!" el Lobo grinned. His mouth was watering as he thought of the rabbit stew. His boca could taste el caldo already.

"No, no, no!" yelled Conejito. "Go away! ¡Vete!"

"Oh, but you will like it, mi amigo," said el señor Lobo.

"¡Vete! I am not your friend!" said the bunny.

14

Lobo was getting mad. He paced above the burrow and thought, "What shall I do? La luna is almost full and I must have conejo stew or I will surely go loco."

Then Lobo saw the chimney. "If he won't come out on his own, I will scare him out!" he thought. Lobo returned with a snake. He dropped la serpiente down la chimenea.

"Come out, amigo, come out before el señor Serpiente bites you!"

"You can't scare me," Conejito laughed.
"This little snake will make a good pet!"

Now el señor Lobo was really mad. In a few hours, la luna would be full. He had to begin cooking the conejo stew at once! Just then, he saw a barrel of cactus molasses.

"Aha!" snarled the wolf. He knew that the molasses from el cactus was very sticky and full of needles. "This will do the trick!" he cheered.

19

Lobo knocked the barrel over and began rolling it down the canyon toward Conejito's burrow. "Heh, heh!" he laughed. "Soon I'll catch you, juicy little conejo. I shall make a most delicious caldo!"

He rolled the barrel on top of the burrow and poured the gooey molasses down la chimenea.

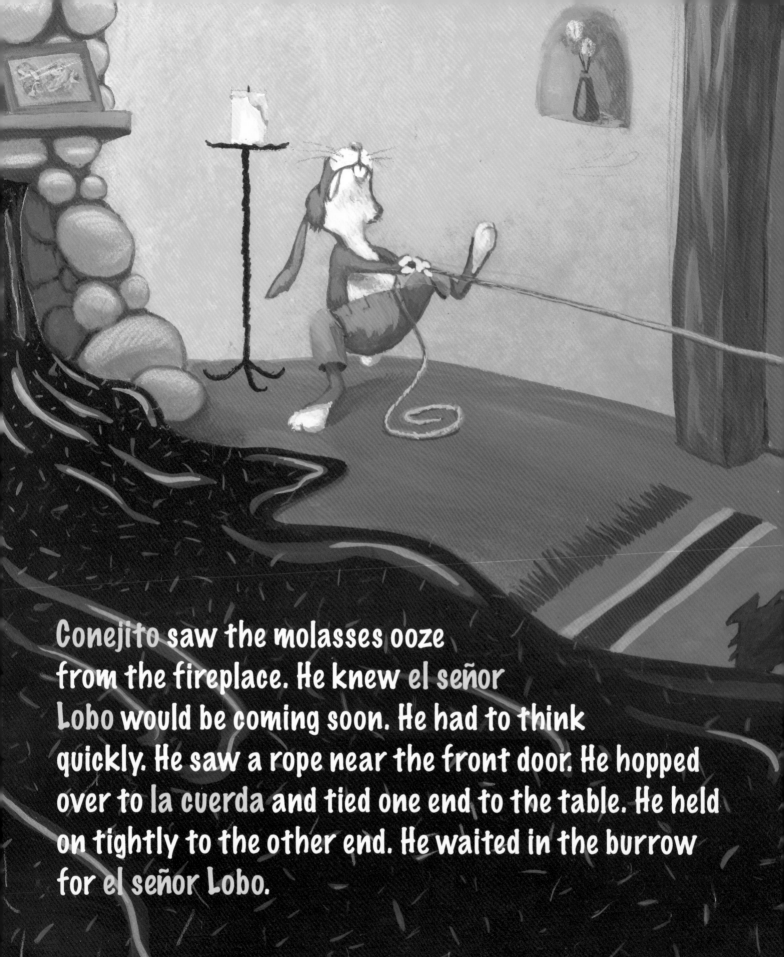

Conejito saw the molasses ooze
from the fireplace. He knew el señor
Lobo would be coming soon. He had to think
quickly. He saw a rope near the front door. He hopped
over to la cuerda and tied one end to the table. He held
on tightly to the other end. He waited in the burrow
for el señor Lobo.

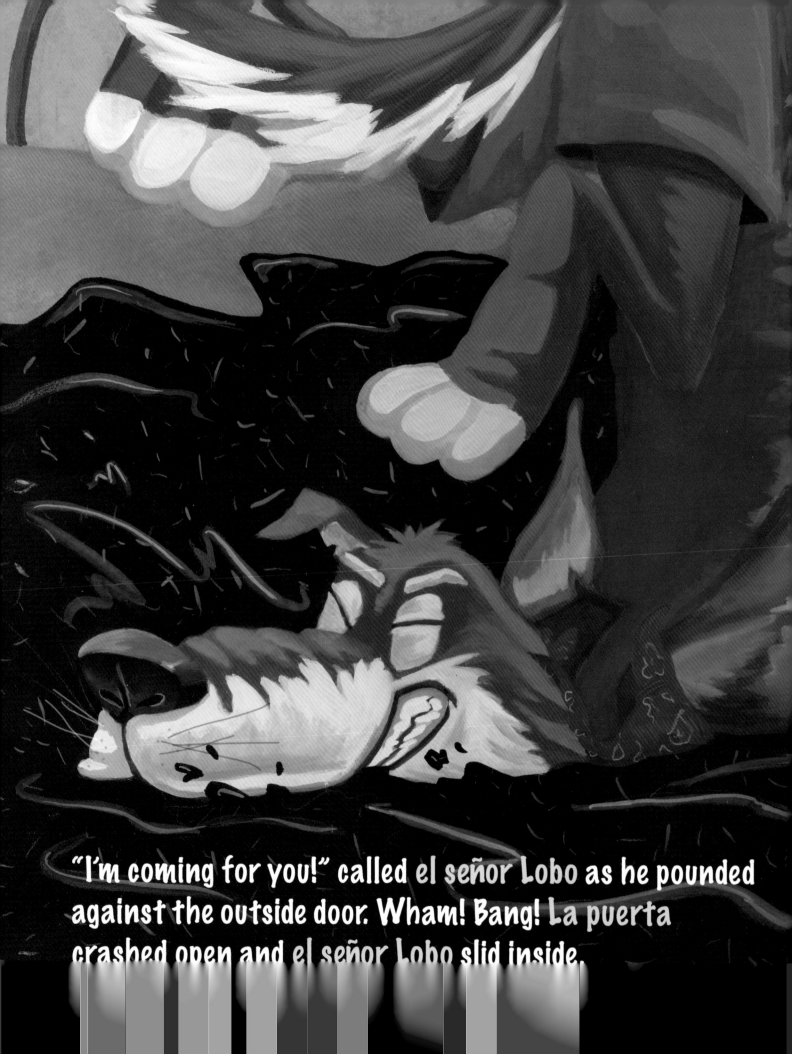

"I'm coming for you!" called el señor Lobo as he pounded against the outside door. Wham! Bang! La puerta crashed open and el señor Lobo slid inside.

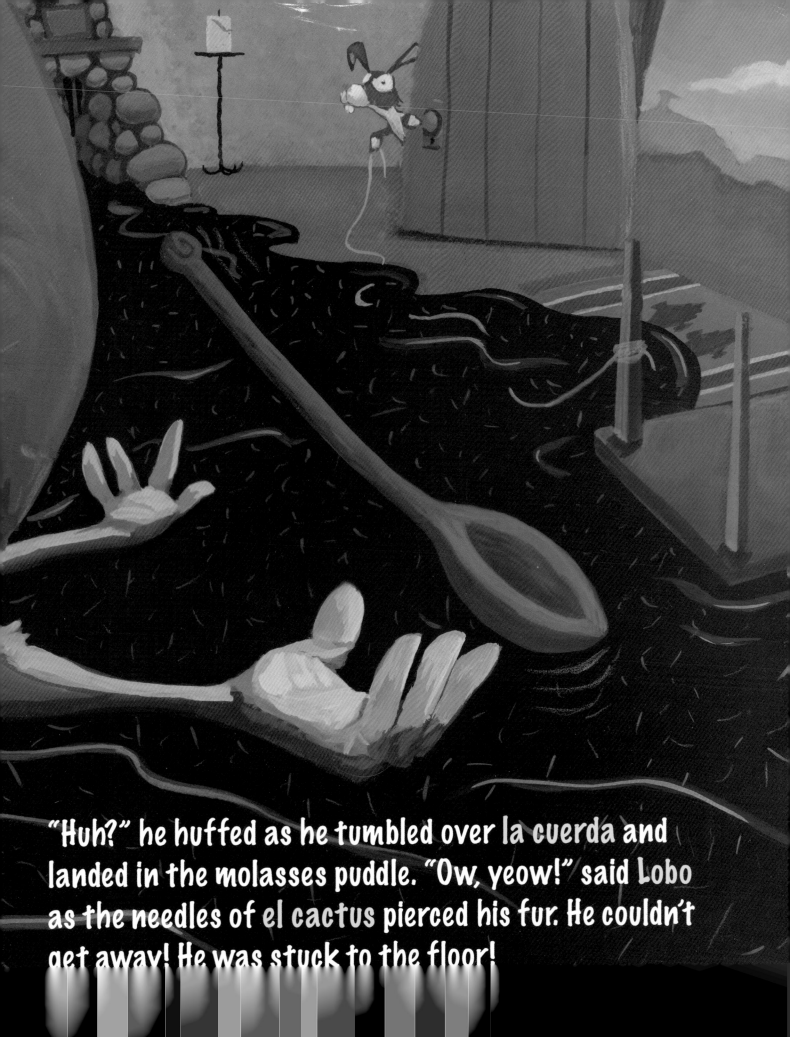

"Huh?" he huffed as he tumbled over la cuerda and landed in the molasses puddle. "Ow, yeow!" said Lobo as the needles of el cactus pierced his fur. He couldn't get away! He was stuck to the floor!

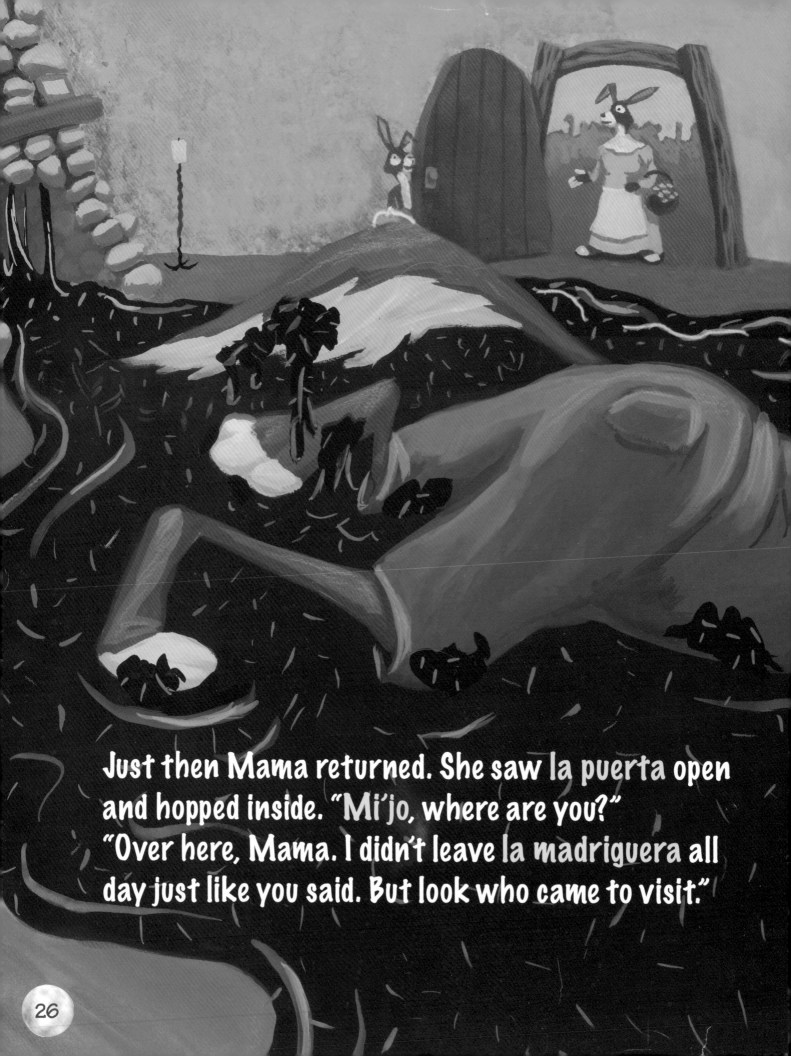

Just then Mama returned. She saw la puerta open and hopped inside. "Mi'jo, where are you?"
"Over here, Mama. I didn't leave la madriguera all day just like you said. But look who came to visit."

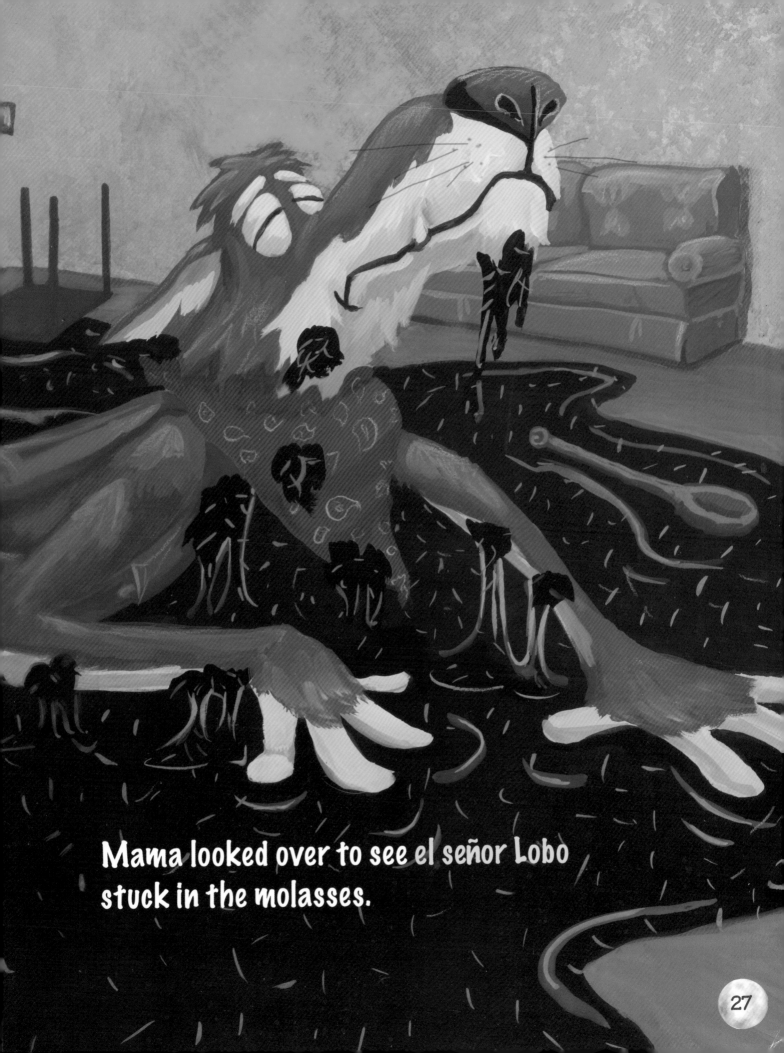

Mama looked over to see el señor Lobo
stuck in the molasses.

"Ha! Ha! Old lobo, you didn't make a rabbit stew out of me!" called Conejito.

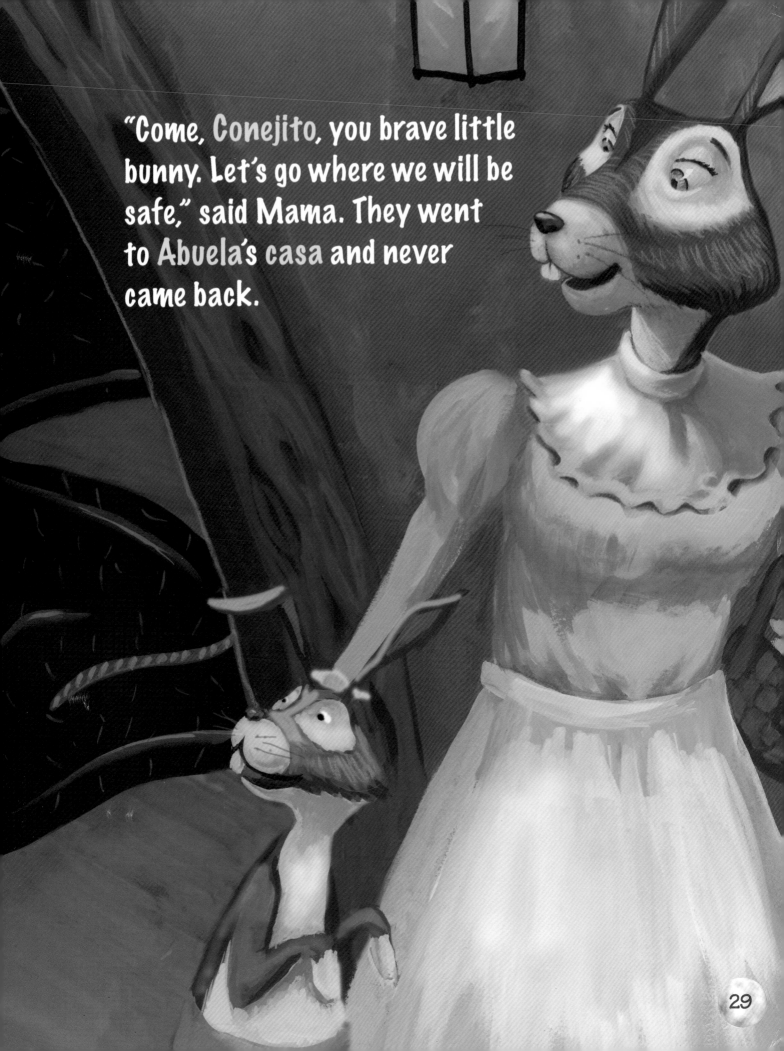

"Come, Conejito, you brave little bunny. Let's go where we will be safe," said Mama. They went to Abuela's casa and never came back.

Meanwhile, old señor Lobo is still plucking cactus thorns from his fur. You'll hear him howling on a clear night when la luna is full.

Vocabulary

mister	el (los) señor(es)
wolf	el (los) lobo(s)
moon	la(s) luna(s)
tomorrow	la(s) mañana(s)
crazy	loco(a)
bunny	el (los) conejito(s)
rabbit	el (los) conejo(s)
burrow	la(s) madriguera(s)
blanket	la(s) manta(s)
grandmother	la(s) abuela(s)
you understand	comprendes
yes	sí
door	la(s) puerta(s)
hello	hola
my	mi(s)
little	el (los) pequeño(s)
friend	el (los) amigo(s)
go	vete
baby	el (los) bebé(s)
very	muy
delicious	delicioso(a)
mouth	la(s) boca(s)
stew	el (los) caldo(s)
snake	la(s) serpiente(s)
chimney	la(s) chimenea(s)
cactus	el (los) cactus
rope	la(s) cuerda(s)
my son	mi'jo
house	la(s) casa(s)

Vocabulario